BOOK 3

Hector Afloat

By Elizabeth Shreeve
Illustrated by Pamela R. Levy

ALADDIN PAPERBACKS
New York London Toronto Sydney

To Barbara, Ben, and Gloria —E. S.

First Aladdin Paperbacks edition May 2004

Text copyright © 2004 by Elizabeth Shreeve
Illustrations copyright © 2004 by Pamela Levy

ALADDIN PAPERBACKS
An imprint of Simon & Schuster
Children's Publishing Division
1230 Avenue of the Americas
New York, NY 10020

Designed by Debra Sfetsios
The text of this book was set in Graham.

Printed in the United States of America
2 4 6 8 10 9 7 5 3 1
Library of Congress Control Number 2003110500
ISBN 0-689-86416-7

The Adventures of Hector Fuller

BOOK 3

Hector Afloat

BOOK 3

Hector Afloat

Table of Contents

Chapter One

Flying Lesson

Rain fell for hours and hours. For days and days. For weeks.

Outside Hector Fuller's wumblebug hole, rain battered the trees and pounded autumn leaves into the mud. Down the hill from his tunnels, the stream rose over its banks and turned the garden into a lake. The lake disappeared into clouds and fog, and the world grew smaller every day.

Hector didn't mind. His snug, little home was full of food. His bookshelf was full of books. He had plenty of company–his cousin Suzy, a plump and lovely ladybug, and his old friend, Lance the lacewing.

And today his new friend, Frederica the

spider, would teach them to spin a web.

"How do you do that?" asked Hector, watching Frederica build an outline made of silk threads as she leaped across the room. "How do you know where to start and which way to go?"

Frederica tightened the striped scarf that she wore around her thin waist. She peered at her work and sighed. "I cannot explain. It just . . . comes to me. This one will be good, don't you think?"

"It's beautiful," said Suzy, who sat in a big chair next to Hector. "Sit down, Lance. Let's watch."

Frederica was a blur now, dancing and darting out from the center of the web to make its spokes. Then she raced in circles, spinning faster and faster to weave a spiral of fine threads across the frame. Finally she sat back and wiped her forehead with one of her eight elegant legs.

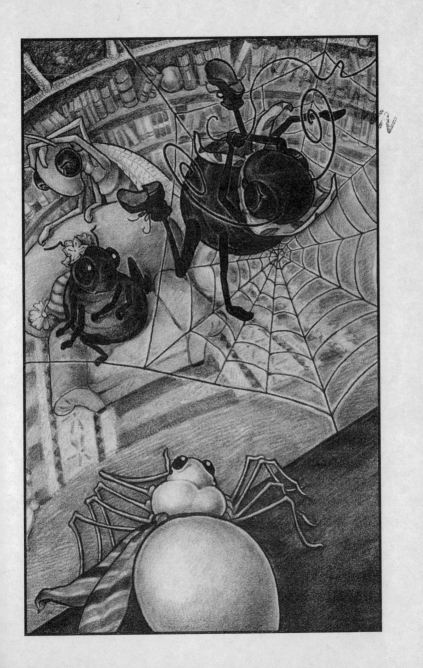

"Wow," said Hector. "I wish I could do that."

Lance shook his wings and laughed. "You? You're a wumblebug, not a spider. Stick to digging tunnels."

"Nonsense," said Frederica. "We are all artists inside. You must picture it in your mind. Like this!" She tossed a silk dragline into the air and floated to the mantelpiece.

"All right." Hector fluttered his short wings and scrambled up next to her. "Here I go!"

Hector took a dragline from Frederica, closed his eyes, and jumped. Halfway across the room, he fell. He bounced off the edge of the web and shot over to the bookshelf, which tipped over and sent a river of books onto the floor. He knocked Suzy off the chair, then slammed down onto the pillows and slid into the fireplace.

Ashes and the stuffing of pillows filled the room.

Suzy and Lance jumped up, coughing and

laughing at the same time. "So much for Hector's career as a spider," said Suzy. "I think we'd better go."

"See you later." Lance opened the door and grinned. "Keep working on the circus act!"

"Good-bye!" called Hector. "Good-bye!" He stood in the tunnel and waved, as rain drummed down on the roof even harder than before.

Chapter Two

Weather Forecast

Back inside Hector's hole, Frederica was starting a new web.

"It's a mess out there," said Hector. "You'd better sleep over. How about I play something on the piano while you spin?"

Frederica turned a circle in the air. "Music! Melody! Harmony!"

Hector smiled. "I only know a couple of songs," he said, and sat down to play, with two legs on the pedals and four more on the keys.

That was as far as he got. For at that moment, someone knocked on the door so hard that it slammed open with a loud bang.

An enormous spider filled the tunnel. He was very hairy and gray with a bushy beard and a long cape with a hood. He had eight different

eyes–two big ones in front, two more looking up, and a row of four small ones below.

The eyes swiveled this way and that. When they spotted Frederica, the spider swept back his cape and bowed.

"Ah, Miss Frederica! How lovely to see ya! May I interest you in something . . . new?"

"Good evening, Wolf," said Frederica. "However did you find me here?"

"Aha!" said the wolf spider in a gruff and growling voice. "My customers are my business, you know. As I always say, 'Door to door, and web to nest . . . we sell nothing but the best! Wolf Spider Products aim to please . . . and let you live a life of ease!'"

Without waiting for an invitation, Wolf squeezed through the doorway into Hector's hole, pulling a big box behind him. His thick, hairy legs moved everywhere as he lifted the lid. Out came drawers and shelves and bottles of all sizes and shapes and colors–yellows and reds, browns and blacks, greens like the grass, and blues like the summer sky. There were packages wrapped in spiderweb, and cobweb baskets full of things that Hector had never seen.

Frederica touched the bottles lightly, as if she did not really care. "Well, perhaps just one . . ."

Wolf grabbed a dozen bottles and set them in a tall pyramid. "Buy two, buy three . . . buy four or five. You need to eat to stay alive! Buy six or seven, eight or ten . . . the flood will come, we don't know when!"

Hector crept closer and looked into a bottle full of bright green juice. Small bits and pieces of things floated around inside. "What do the different colors mean?" he asked. "What's this one?"

Wolf chuckled again. "Buy green or yellow, red or blue . . . find the one that's right for you! Buy a bundle wrapped up tight. . . . The water will rise high tonight!"

"We won't flood here," said Hector. "There's been a wumblebug hole here for ages, and it's never flooded yet."

"There's a first for everything, wumblebug!

Before you sleep, roll up the rug!" Wolf held out a clump of plant stems, wrapped in silk. "For our insect friends . . . choose any length. Guaranteed to give you strength! All are sweet and make you strong . . . when it's raining all night long!"

Frederica picked out the green bottle and the juiciest bunch of stems. "We'll take these," she said.

Wolf bowed. "Then I shall bid you both farewell. What the storm will bring, we cannot tell!" In an instant he had packed his cart, squeezed back through the doorway, and disappeared up the tunnel.

"What is all this stuff, anyway?" said Hector. The stems looked delicious to him. "Is it paint?"

"Mmmm . . . no." Frederica sniffed her bottle. "You see, a spider like myself cannot spend time chasing food. Yes?"

"Yes. I mean, no. Aren't spiders supposed to catch things to eat?"

"Let us say that I am more interested in food

for the soul. So Wolf provides a most convenient product."

"You mean," said Hector, "the juice in there is spider food? As in . . . bugs?"

Frederica waved her long legs. "Even an artist must eat. Wumblebugs are not appetizing, but some of your friends . . ."

"Right." Suddenly Hector did not feel hungry at all. "Well, we'd better get some sleep. You take my bed. I'll sleep out here."

Frederica glided away, holding the bottle tightly.

Hector tucked himself deep into his soft chair. Just before he fell asleep, he took a last look around the room. There was his old piano with sheets of music waiting on the stand. In the morning he would play for Frederica while she wove another web.

Outside the rain still fell. The stream rose higher and faster, and water crept up the hill.

Chapter Three

Flood

Hector dreamed that he was floating in a cloud and the cloud was wet, and that Lance was hitting him on the head with a book.

Hector opened his eyes. Everything was dark. Through the tunnel came a noise he'd never heard–a whooshing sound, like wind under the ground. His big chair rocked back and forth. A painting of his grandmother banged against the wall.

Hector sprang from the chair and landed in water that went up to his six knees. Things floated and bumped in the dark–pots and pans from the kitchen, the piano bench, books. The whooshing sound grew louder, as if wind was tearing and grinding at the earth.

Only it wasn't wind. It couldn't be wind. It had to be a flood.

"No!" cried Hector as if the water would hear him. "Stop!"

He ran toward the bedroom. Frederica rushed out. They crashed into each other in the dark as a wave burst the door open and poured into Hector's hole.

"Hold on to the piano!" Hector dragged Frederica to the piano, and they both grabbed on to it, bracing themselves against the flood.

It was no use. The wave lifted everything in its way–the kitchen, the fireplace . . . even the walls. Water picked up Hector's home and tossed it aside, carrying Hector and Frederica away like specks in the wind.

"Hang on!" Hector cried.

"I'm trying!" answered Frederica. They rode the piano out of the hill and down to the stream, under the beating rain. Another wave hit them, then another from the opposite side.

Suddenly Frederica was gone.

Hector cried out. He reached for Frederica and the piano slipped from his grasp. He thrashed his legs and wings to stay afloat. He fluttered and flopped and grabbed blindly at the tops of bushes as the stream swept him along.

His legs caught hold of a branch. For a moment he clung on to it, shivering and numb. Then he pulled himself onto a twig.

At the top of the branch were some leaves— or *some*thing—that kept the rain off his head. Below him the water rushed by, taking his home away. If it did not rise any higher, he might be safe for the night.

As for Frederica—or Suzy or Lance—he might not ever know.

Chapter Four

Baby Turtle

Hector did not sleep much. He clung to the branch and watched the night fade away. Finally the rain stopped and the sun came up over the flood. Water stretched in all directions—too wide for a wumblebug to fly across and much too fast to swim.

Hector looked up. Something was still there, but it wasn't leaves. It was a turtle. A baby snapping turtle, clamped to the branch with her mouth. Hector climbed closer until he could see her whole body, from her square head to her skinny slip of a tail. Her brown shell was tangled in the stems of a water lily, and her legs pointed straight out to the sides.

"Are you stuck?" called Hector.

The snapping turtle nodded without letting go of the branch.

"Would you like me to undo the knots?"

She nodded again, so hard that the whole branch wobbled.

Hector climbed up toward her. Then he stopped. "You won't . . . do anything while I'm working, will you?"

The snapping turtle shook her head.

Hector began to untie the stems one by one, starting with the smallest ones. "Let me guess," he said as he worked. "You tried to get loose and just got more tangled up?"

She nodded as he slipped through the last tangle. The water lilies dropped onto the fast water below. "There you are," he said after he flew a safe distance below. The turtle grunted but did not let go. "What's that–you're scared? Well, you can't stay up there forever. Try one little step down."

The turtle moved a teeny bit, then chomped

back on to the branch.

"C'mon now, a little farther!" said Hector. "You need to be brave. Think of all that mud down there waiting for you. . . ."

She took a big step toward Hector and grabbed back on to the branch so hard that she snapped it off. *Kersplash!* Into the water she fell.

She popped back up with a splash. "Oh, turtle!" she yelled. "Hey, call me Henriette. What's your name? You're the best untangler ever! Ever, ever, ever!"

"I'm Hector." He watched her flip and wiggle and dive in the water until he had to laugh. "Was it worth getting stuck up there, just for something to eat?"

"You bet!" said Henriette. "The last flowers of the summer are the tastiest of all! Snapping turtles love to eat, you know. Eat, eat, eat! We eat everything, and now we'll eat even more!"

"Why's that?" asked Hector.

"Because water belongs to snapping turtles,

and now the whole world is water. So everything belongs to us. Isn't that great?"

"But what about everyone else?"

Henriette splished-sploshed in a circle and ended with a somersault. "Don't worry. Somebody handy like you can always work for us. Hop on! You're coming home with me."

At the mention of home Hector felt tired and sad. The turtle could swim away to her family. She even carried a house on her back. The wumblebug hole was gone forever. His friends were scattered and lost.

But if he stayed on the branch, he would starve.

He crept onto the top of Henriette's head.

"I'm hungry," she said as she began to swim. "Did I mention that?"

"Well, don't eat me," Hector mumbled.

"Not a chance! You're red, and red bugs taste bad, bad, bad! What do you eat that makes you taste so bad?"

"Plants, mostly."

"Mmm, plants are yummy! I could never eat enough plants. Or not-plants either. Plants and not-plants! Plants and not-plants! Want to hear my song?" Henriette began to sing as she swam, splashing extra at the end of each line.

"Duckweed, pondweed, crabs or leeches,
anything within our reaches!
Frogs or snakes, all sorts of fishes.
We don't stop to wash the dishes!
Spider, worm, or lizard's head,
we love it all, alive or dead!
We're snapping turtles, don't you see?
And we are always hun-gar-eee!"

"Do you like it?" she said, finishing off her song with a big spray of water that soaked Hector from his antennae to the tips of his wings.

"It certainly gets the point across," said

Hector. "Are all snapping turtles like you?"

"Bigger, bigger, bigger! We start out small but the more we eat, the bigger we get. So let's hurry and get to headquarters for lunch!"

Henriette began to swim faster, and Hector had to hold on tight.

Chapter Five

Snappers

urtle headquarters was nothing but a vast puddle of shallow water and logs jammed into the mud. Turtles of all sizes–mostly huge–floated around looking like islands. They stared as Henriette paddled by, and it seemed to Hector that they were staring in a hungry way.

Henriette swam straight ahead without looking right or left. "It's a mess, huh?" she whispered. "Our old headquarters got washed out, and everybody's in a bad mood."

"Where are we going?" Hector asked.

"To Grandpa. To get you a job. You can fix anything, right?"

"Not really. I don't have my tools, and–"

"Better say you can," said Henriette, "because here we are."

She stopped in front of a big log. Three giant turtles sat basking on top of it, watching them through half-closed eyes. Their great jaws hooked like the beaks of hawks. Their skin was warty and rough.

"Good morning, Grandpa!" Henriette sang out. "I brought a special guest."

"Run along, Henriette," said Grandpa, who was the biggest turtle. The skin at his throat hung in scaly wrinkles that wobbled when he talked. "We're flooded. There's no place for guests."

"No place for anyone," grumbled another of the giant turtles. "Whole families without a place to sleep."

"Seems to me," said the third, who was only slightly smaller, "that we need to build some sleeping platforms and some–"

"We already did," said the medium-size turtle. "Your boys got to fighting and bit 'em to pieces and–"

"Those were your sister's kids, sure as my shell!"

"Enough!" Grandpa Turtle spoke in a loud, booming voice. "Henriette, this is no time for guests."

"But he can fix anything," Henriette said. "Anything at all!"

The turtles stretched out their necks and looked more closely at Henriette's head.

"It's a bug," said the second turtle.

"We eat bugs," said the third.

Henriette ignored them and smiled at her grandpa. "You should have seen him! There I was, swimming along, when this monster jumped out of the water, like this . . ." She stood up and flung out her front legs. "I fought like crazy but it got me. Then this bug comes surfing on this big wave and he jumps"–Henriette leaped out of the water, so that Hector nearly fell off–"and then he does this thing with his little antennae-feelers or something and saves me completely and otherwise I'd still be stuck, stuck, stuck!"

Grandpa Turtle sighed. "Henriette, what am I going to do with you? Whoever heard of a– what is it, a wumblebug?–living with snapping turtles?"

"Please, Grandpa! Please, please, please!" Henriette used a sweet voice that Hector had not yet heard from her. "He's got lots of uses. I promise."

The medium-size giant butted the smaller one with his head. "More uses than your boys, I'll bet."

"Now, wait just a minute . . ." The smaller giant lumbered to his feet.

Grandpa stood up first. He frowned at the others. "All right, all right. Henriette, take him to the beach. He can clean up . . . after somebody's kids."

"You're the best!" yelled Henriette, and she splashed off before any more giant turtles could say a word.

Chapter Six

Lily Pad

Hector and Henriette swam to a muddy beach at the edge of the floodwater. Broken stuff lay everywhere. Henriette pulled up to a tall pile of wood and broken sticks tangled with vines. Hector climbed off.

"Here you go!" she said. "Lots and lots of untangling, just right for a bug like you. Didn't I promise to get you a job?"

"Yes," said Hector. "But . . ."

"Hey, you've got to work if you want to eat," said Henriette. "Right? Speaking of which . . . I'm off to lunch. I'll see you later, later, later!" She turned and paddled away.

Hector slumped down on the pile. He could work his whole life and never make a dent in

this mess. And what kind of life would it be? Working for snapping turtles that broke everything they got near? Who might forget and gobble him up?

Rain began to fall again, first as a drizzle and then in a steady stream. Hector climbed off the pile and tried to dig a hole to get out of the cool air and the wetness. The hole filled with water and slurped into the mud.

Hector looked up and down the beach. Everything was muddy and gray and dark. Everything except for a clump of mushrooms, poking up from the mud like a forest of colors—yellow and orange, with red spots on top.

Hector dashed over and huddled under the mushroom caps. They were slimy and cold, but they made a roof over his head.

All afternoon he sat thinking of home and watching the floodwater lap at the shore. He thought of his friends as raindrops plopped into circles on puddles. After a while he just sat and did not think at all.

Evening came and the rain stopped. A clump of lily pads floated by. The smallest one bumped up against the shore as if inviting him for a ride.

Hector shivered and stood up. He walked to the water's edge and stepped onto the lily pad–first his front feet, then the middle ones, then the back. The lily pad wobbled but floated, steady and firm. An evening breeze rose from the shore and caught the lily pad, sending it off into the night with Hector aboard.

Chapter Seven

Shipshape

Hector woke up unsure of where he was and how he had gotten there.

The morning fog swirled over the water all around. There was no horizon. No shadows. No edges to anything. The lily pad drifted in circles on a cloud of water and mist.

A white-and-pink flower floated by. Hector reached out and pulled it aboard. It was broken and bruised but smelled sweet. *Henriette would like it,* thought Hector. *She would gobble it up.*

Hector smiled and realized that he was hungry too. He nibbled on the flower. Not bad. Not bad at all. He munched and munched, feeling stronger with every bite.

More flowers came bobbing through the

mist, along with some twigs–two long ones and one short. Hector set the flowers aside and lined up the twigs. Then he looked more closely at the lily pad.

It was wide and strong, with a rib down the middle and smaller ones out to the sides. In the back the leaf had a deep notch where the stub of the stem hung down.

Hector picked up the shortest stick and jammed one end into the stem. If he moved it back and forth, he could use it as a tiller to steer. Then he stuck the other two sticks through the leaf's tough edges. He could row and steer at the same time. The lily pad would be a good boat.

But where would he go?

Hector's thoughts stretched out over the water. He watched the sun shine through the mist and shimmer across the waves. The sun had been at his back when he traveled on Henriette's head. If he headed the opposite way, he would find whatever was left of his home. Maybe even a friend.

Hector turned his boat into the morning light. He began to row–two legs to stand, two to paddle, one for the tiller, and one to keep the sun out of his eyes. The lily pad rocked gently forward and the morning sun grew brighter. Paddle, swing. Paddle, swing. Hector thought of Henriette again and began to hum a song.

"Paddle, swing. Paddle, swing.
Stretch your feelers, flap your wing!
Water splashing all around,
paddle till you run aground!"

It was a short song so he sang it over and over. He pulled at the oars again and again. His legs began to ache, and the ache in his legs made him forget the sadness in his heart.

Chapter Eight

Message in a Bottle

Hector paddled and the sun burned the fog into patches over the water. Sunshine peeked through for a moment; then mist whirled back like curtains closing. When it opened again, Hector saw two bright pieces of color floating toward him. He stopped rowing and pulled them in.

They were bottles–the wolf spider's bottles. One was bright purple. The other was red. Hector drained their contents into the water and set them down with his flowers.

What could a wumblebug do with a bottle? Hector nibbled on a blossom and thought of Henriette. He missed her. Without her he would still be stuck on the stick. He would send her a note.

Hector laid out the largest flower petal and began to scratch out some words.

Dear Henree-yet,
   Here's a snack.
        Hector

He slipped the petal inside one of the bottles, plugged the top with a piece of leaf, and threw it over the side.

The mist billowed and blew away. Suddenly Hector could see sunshine and shadows again. Just for fun, he stood up and waved a paddle in the air. A shadow paddle waved back. Then another shadow caught his eye–the shadow of a stick jutting out of the water. From the stick hung a spider's web, a lopsided web that drooped in the middle. And next to the web, all scrunched up, was a spider with a torn and muddy scarf around her waist.

"Frederica!" Hector shouted and waved his

paddle again. The spider did not look up.

The fog crept back. Before it cut off his view, Hector saw something else–the dark head of a snake, swimming around the stick.

A water snake, circling its prey before it struck.

Chapter Nine

Setting Sail

"**F**rederica, wake up! Watch out! There's a snake!" Hector yelled as loudly as he could. Through the mist came a small splash. Maybe the snake was breaking out of the water and slithering up the stick. Maybe not far away.

Hector grabbed the longest paddle and held it up in the air as high as he could reach.

"Frederica! Throw a line!"

"Where?" Her voice came out of the fog. "I can't see you!"

"Here!" Hector reached higher still and waved the paddle like a flag. In that instant the sun broke through. The snake struck. And Frederica threw a dragline and leaped.

Thump! Frederica landed smack on Hector's

head. They sprawled out flat on the lily pad and slid across, almost into the water.

Hector scrambled to his feet. He grabbed the paddles and began to row, and they slipped away into the mist.

"Thank you," said Frederica in a small voice. She did not look well.

"You spiders are amazing," said Hector. "Have you been on that stick all this time?"

Frederica nodded.

"Have you gotten anything to eat?"

Frederica shook her head and looked sadly at the empty bottle at Hector's feet.

"Sorry," said Hector. "It's empty and it's the only one. Don't you think you'd better catch something?"

Frederica sank lower into the lily pad.

Hector took a few more strokes and stopped. He pulled the paddles in and up over the lily pad so that they crossed over his head. Then he wrapped the handles together with Frederica's dragline.

"There you go," he said. "I'm no good at webs, remember? It's up to you."

"No, no," said Frederica. "How will you paddle?"

"We're not going anywhere," said Hector, "until you eat."

Frederica's legs shook as she stood up. She trembled as she climbed up onto the paddles and spun a slow spiral from one stick to another. Then she lay back in the corner to wait.

Hector sat at the tiller and pretended not to watch.

A swarm of tiny gnats flew over the water's surface and got caught in the web. Frederica climbed over and bit them to make them sleep, wrapped them in silk, and sucked each one of them dry.

"You know," said Hector as if nothing had happened, "I once knew a baby spiderling. For a few minutes, anyway. She gave me a ride

from a very tall tree. But we didn't have much time to talk."

Frederica gave a tiny burp and wiped her mouth. "Why not?"

"You might say she caught a different breeze. I never saw her again."

Frederica looked down and smiled. "You seemed much bigger, then."

"It was you?" Hector laughed. "Why . . . good thing I rescued you! We'd never have figured it out."

"And now," said Frederica, "we shall drift together forever. How tragic! How sad!"

Hector laughed again. But it was true–they were moving slowly without the paddles. The wind was behind them, but the breeze whistled right through the web.

"Do you suppose . . . do you think you could fill it in there a bit?" Hector said, pointing to a big hole in the web. Frederica climbed up the paddles again and began to spin. "Perfect. And there . . . a little more on the side . . . good. Now let's see."

Frederica wove this way and that until the web turned into a sail. The sail filled with wind. The boat gained speed. Hector held firm to the tiller, and Frederica's scarf fluttered behind her in the breeze.

Off they sailed, the wumblebug and the spider, over the endless water that covered everything they knew.

Chapter Ten

Ahoy

They sailed all day, moving fast with a stiff breeze. By sunset the sky was clear. Frederica and Hector lay on the lily pad and looked up as stars spread above them in a broad band.

"So distant! So far!" said Frederica. "The lonely, lonely stars!"

"No more than usual, I suppose," said Hector. "But it does seem like a big world tonight. I wonder . . ."

"What?"

"I wonder if there will be anything left." Hector's voice shook a little. "If . . . if I'll ever have a wumblebug hole again."

"Of course you will!" said Frederica. "Look at me–I build a new home every day. I was born to spin, Hector. You were born to dig."

"I don't know," said Hector. "I should have thought more. . . . I should have done more. . . ."

"No one knows everything."

Hector shook his head. "Wolf knew the flood was coming. I just didn't want to listen. Maybe I could have kept us from getting washed away. I could have been brave."

"But you rescued me!"

"I wasn't brave, though. I was scared."

"You can be both, I think," said Frederica. "Do you know what spiders do? Before they jump they make a safety thread."

"Well," said Hector, "so far my safety thread is nothing but luck."

The wind died down, and the waves rocked Hector and Frederica to sleep. When they woke, the sky was blue, and the sail was dotted with fat drops. Frederica spun a new web and Hector used the old one to scoop up plants for breakfast. Then they steered the boat straight into the morning sun until something made Hector turn.

"What is it?" asked Frederica.

Hector didn't answer. He was listening to a sound, sort of a *plink* or a *plunk*. Something familiar and also very far away. "There!" he said finally and thrust the tiller hard to one side so that the lily pad tilted on its edge and headed upwind. They sailed past a few trees sticking up out of the water. The flood was starting to recede.

A tiny island came into view. They sailed closer and saw someone or something on the shore. Hector steered as close as he could until a thick layer of weeds pulled the lily pad to a stop.

"Ahoy!" cried Hector.

"Hi!"

"Hello!"

Hector's heart leaped. He knew those voices as well as his own. They belonged to his old friend, Lance, and his favorite cousin, Suzy the ladybug.

"Need a ride?" he called.

"Yes!" they called back. "But you come here first!"

"Why?"

They waved but did not answer.

Hector stepped off the lily pad and onto the weeds. *Glop. Slurp.* The plants grabbed his legs and pulled him in. *Glug. Gloop.* He fluttered his wings, rose a little, and took another step, faster and faster across the water. When he reached the island, he was sopping wet.

Suzy and Lance sat on a rock and watched with enormous smiles.

"What," Hector said, panting, "are you doing here? Why didn't you fly away?"

"It's too far to fly anywhere," said Lance. "We might not have found a place to land."

"Plus," said Suzy, "we thought you might want this." She and Lance hopped down from the rock.

Only it wasn't a rock. It was Hector's piano, missing one leg and wrapped all around with weeds.

Chapter Eleven

Big Mouths

"**W**here did you find it?" Hector cried. "How did you get it here? Does it still play? What happened to–"

"Hold on," said Lance. "The real question is: What do we do now?"

"Right," said Hector. "Let's see. Might be too heavy for the boat . . ."

"What boat?" Suzy asked.

Hector turned and pointed to the lily pad. Frederica waved to them from high atop the sail.

"Wonderful!" said Suzy. "Now wait a minute . . . let me see . . ." She marched down to the water and returned with a huge bundle of weeds. She pulled off the little hollow balls that grew under the stems and began to weave the plants into a net.

Hector and Lance watched.

"What are those?" Lance pointed to the hollow balls.

"These?" Suzy held some of them up. "That's what makes the plants float. We'll wrap them along the edges of the net. Then we'll put it under the piano and tie this long piece behind the boat."

"It's good," said Hector. "If it works. Sort of a combination raft-net."

"Are you kidding? It's great!" said Lance. "C'mon! Let's give it a try."

They lifted the piano out of the mud. Suzy slid the net underneath it, and they pulled the whole thing, step by step, into the water. The piano bobbed and floated as if waiting for a ride.

"Yo-ho!" yelled Lance. "Ho-ho! Or what do sailors say?"

Hector laughed. "How about 'full speed ahead'?"

They fluttered to the boat and crowded

aboard. Frederica tied the net to the stern of the lily pad and hoisted a new sail. Hector took his place at the tiller and they sailed downwind, pulling the piano behind.

Frederica perched on her web. "I shall ride up here, as the deck is rather full."

"Hey, Lance," said Suzy. "Get your foot off my wing."

"Huh? Oh, sorry," said Lance. "You know, this boat is great. How does that tiller work, anyway?" He stood up. The boat tilted and nearly capsized.

"Sit down!" shouted Hector. "Sit right there in the middle, with your head down so I can see. Now, look. The tiller attaches to the rudder, which is the part that's in the water. In this case–the stem. And this–"

"And what's that?" Suzy pointed off the side of the boat.

The water around them swished and spun. A fin broke the surface, then a great mouth with whiskers sticking out of each side. Shiny scales flashed silver and gold. Another and another, circling around them, until the water seemed as if it were boiling.

They were sailing in a sea filled with hungry fish.

Chapter Twelve

Fish Chase

The three bugs and the spider froze with fear. Wherever they looked, there were fish. Thrashing. Swarming. Sucking in water and anything else they found.

Hector shouted the first thing that came into his head.

"Frederica, more sail! Spin, spin! Suzy and Lance, hold on to the back and fly. Faster! Faster! As fast as you can!"

Frederica leaped into action, spinning furiously until the whole top of the boat was a wind-filled sail. Suzy and Lance flapped their wings. The lily pad sprang forward and sped over the water like a leaf in a storm wind. Hector thrust the tiller this way and that, slipping over the

sides of fish and dodging their gaping mouths.

Away they flew, with the piano airborne in its net. The fish chased them from behind.

The landscape began to change. Even in the rush, Hector saw things he knew. Trees. Rocks. The world was coming out of the flood, covered with mud.

"Hey," Lance called. "Isn't that–"

"The stream," cried Hector. "Yes! Keep flying!"

The boat picked up speed as the floodwater rushed into the stream. The current snatched everything up in its flow–the fish, the boat, broken pieces left from the flood. Suddenly Hector knew where they were.

He steered straight for a gravel bank at the side of the stream.

"Watch out!" Suzy shouted. "We'll crash!"

Hector held his course. Head down, legs on the tiller, antennae straight ahead.

"When I say the word," he called, "everyone up in the air! Ready . . . now!"

They hit the bank. The three bugs flew.

Frederica threw a dragline and jumped. The lily pad, still pulling the piano, skimmed over the bank and landed in a pool of water perched high in the rocks, leaving the swarm of fish behind.

Except that an even bigger fish was waiting for them.

Chapter Thirteen

A Stitch in Time

The fish–a carp–lay on its side in the pool, a small whirlpool left from the flood.

The water circled around and around. The boat and the piano circled too. Hector and the others landed back onboard.

"Uhh at!" grunted the carp. "Ooo aaking ee ii-eeey!"

"What's that?" Hector said.

Frederica leaned her head in thought. "I believe . . . I believe he means to say that we're making him dizzy."

"Is he speaking fish-ish?" asked Hector.

"No, no. Although I am rather good with languages." Frederica adjusted her scarf. "He is simply unable to move his mouth."

The carp nodded. A large tear rolled out of his always-open eye.

"Oh. Sorry," said Hector. "What's the matter?"

"Ah-um eeer aa wargh uh rrarm. Uk-uk owk uguuu aarrk! Eek? Aaak eek owk!"

Frederica translated again. "He says he came into this pool because the water was nice and warm, but he tore his mouth on something sharp, became weak, and could not get out."

"Maybe it's a trick," whispered Suzy.

"Let's get out of here," said Lance.

Hector surveyed the pool. The rocks were too steep to climb and too high to fly over. Over the gravel bank, the fish still swarmed in the stream.

"No," Hector said. "We'll have to fix his mouth."

Lance stared. "Fix him? Why?"

"Because–believe it or not–he may be our last hope."

"Our last something," grumbled Lance. "I

don't see how some hungry fish–"

"Frederica, you could do it." Hector swung the boat closer to the carp.

"Do you mean to say," said Frederica, "that you wish me to sew up this large creature's mouth? Will it not eat me as a tiny snack?"

Hector leaned over the carp's sore mouth. "You can sew these two edges," he said. "There . . . and there. See?"

"Aannk-ooo. Oouuuk . . . aaah iiieee urrrek," said the carp. "Ah eik eek-oo."

"Oh dear," said Frederica, moving back. "Oh goodness. Oh my."

"What did he say?" said Lance.

"He said he would appreciate our help but he often forgets, and we'll have to excuse him if he eats us by mistake."

"Never trust a carp," said Lance. "Dumbest fish in the stream."

Hector steered the boat onto a soft patch of dirt near the carp's head. He jumped ashore

and grabbed a stick, lined himself up with the great creature's eye, and began to scratch a note in the mud.

Note to Self:
Ugh!
Bugs taste bad. Spiders too.
Not food.

He stepped back to inspect the message. "That should work. He's all yours, Frederica."

With every leg shaking, the spider climbed onto the carp's whiskers and down into its great mouth. She bit tiny holes into the torn parts of his mouth, one at a time.

The carp began to snore.

Frederica trembled.

The carp's mouth began to open and close.

Hector banged him on the nose with the stick and pointed to the message.

The fish jerked awake.

Frederica threaded silk through each hole and tied them up until at last the wound was repaired. She climbed back onto the boat.

"Yyyyessss!" cried the carp. "Thanks! Uuh . . . who did you say you were?"

"We didn't," said Hector. "But we would like to ask–"

"Hey–where'd the water go?" The carp wriggled around in the mud. "There was water here. Where'd it go?"

"The flood, you see," said Hector. "It's draining away. Now, like I was saying–"

"So how am I supposed to swim, huh? I can't swim in mud."

"Tell you what." Hector steered the lily pad toward the carp's glimmering tail. "There's lots and lots of water just over that bank. Now that you're feeling better, you give one big jump, and I'll bet–"

Ka-boing! The carp did not wait for another word. Arching his shining body, he threw himself over the shallows and into the rushing stream. At the last moment his tail caught the lily pad and flipped it high over the pool.

The tattered leaf cleared the rock cliffs and fell to pieces in midair, sending paddles and piano and passengers to all sides. The sail wrapped around Hector so that he could not flap his wings, and he flew through the air like a little package, up onto dry land.

Chapter Fourteen

Rainbow

"Ahh!" cried Suzy and Lance as they caught the air in their wings and fluttered down.

"Oohhhh!" cried Frederica as she spun a dragline and floated over them.

"Uunck!" grunted Hector as he crashed with a thud.

Cling! Clang! Ching! The piano landed next to him.

Suzy and Lance and Frederica hurried over. "Hector! Are you okay?"

"I'm fine." Hector's voice was muffled by the sail. "Just kind of wrapped up."

Pinch! Snip! Frederica cut him loose. They pulled him out and set the piano on its legs. Then they all sat and looked around.

They were on top of a dry hill that had not been touched by the flood. Below were the stream and the garden and beyond that, the woods. All the places they knew, all covered with mud.

The pale autumn sun peeked out from the clouds. A soft rain began to fall; only a mist, but enough to wash things off.

"Look," said Suzy, pointing toward the setting sun. There, over the garden, was the first hint of a rainbow arching between the clouds.

"Let's go," said Lance. "We'll get something to eat. Hector, you coming?"

Hector shook his head. "You go on," he said. "I need to stay here for a while."

And he did. He stood very still, feeling the dry ground underfoot, watching his friends run downhill under the many-colored bands of light. Then a noise came from behind, and he turned to see the wolf spider panting up the other side of the hill.

"Hello!" Hector called. "Where's all your stuff?"

Wolf stopped and grinned. "Ah . . . the wumblebug! Don't you agree–a most remarkable, miraculous, meteorological event! Indeed, indeed. Wherever I went it was raining! And flooding! I was soaked. I was wet! I've lost my equipment, it's true. And yet . . ."

"That's too bad." Hector remembered the bright bottles floating through the fog. He stood up and hunted around among the remains of the boat. There was Wolf's bottle, still unbroken. "Look! This is yours, I think."

Wolf gave a cry of delight. "Why, thank you, thank you! Of all my bottles, this one is the last. No matter. No matter. It's all in the past! I still have eight legs attached to me. I have eight eyes, so I can see. It's not what you own that counts, you know. It's what you've got inside! Good-bye!"

The wolf spider swept back his muddy cape

and bowed, then continued up the hill toward the woods.

The light was fading now. The rain was gone and the air smelled fresh and new. Suzy and Lance would be finding plenty to eat in the garden. Frederica would be spinning a new web.

Hector Fuller kicked the dirt. His front legs tingled as he found a good soft place.

The time had come to dig.

Elizabeth Shreeve grew up in a family of writers and scientists who taught her to chase butterflies and otherwise scare the daylights out of small creatures in the local marshes and fields. She also liked to read and would have become a librarian if books could be stored outdoors. A graduate of Harvard College and the Harvard Graduate School of Design, she balances a career in environmental design with writing stories and reading in silly voices to her husband and sons. The origin of Hector Fuller's name and species is a closely-held family secret that Elizabeth is happy to share at book signings and school visits, where she talks with children about the natural world, the life of a writer, and the joys of becoming a life-long reader.